GHOSTS OF THE DEEP

GHOSTS OF THE DEEP

DANIEL COHEN

G. P. PUTNAM'S SONS   NEW YORK

G. P. Putnam's Sons, a division of The Putnam & Grosset Group,
200 Madison Avenue, New York, NY 10016.
Published simultaneously in Canada.
Printed in the United States of America.
Book design by Patrick Collins.

Library of Congress Cataloging-in-Publication data

Cohen, Daniel, 1936–   Ghosts of the deep/Daniel Cohen.   p.   cm.
Summary: A collection of encounters with ghostly sailors and
other nautical apparitions.
1. Apparitions—Juvenile literature. 2. Ghosts—Juvenile literature.
3. Sea-stories—Juvenile literature. 4. Shipwrecks—Miscellanea—
Juvenile literature. [1. Ghosts. 2. Supernatural. 3. Sea stories.
4. Shipwrecks.] I. Title.
BF1486.C64   1993   133.1—dc20   92-34669   CIP   AC
ISBN 0-399-22435-1

10   9   8   7   6   5   4   3   2   1

First Impression

For Empress of Blandings

Contents

My Very Own Ghost (Almost)

I have been collecting and writing ghostly accounts for more years than I care to recall. As a result, I am often asked, "Have you ever seen a ghost?"

Generally I look down, shuffle my feet a bit and finally admit that no, I have not. I have tried. Heaven knows I have tried. I have certainly been in more allegedly haunted houses than most people. Sometimes it seems as if everyone I meet has seen a ghost, and I begin to wonder if the spirits have something against me personally.

Not long ago my wife and I spent a few days in the resort town of Cape May, New Jersey. It's a very old town, known primarily for its fine old Victorian houses, many of which have been converted into bed-and-breakfast guest houses. But the town is also on the Atlantic Ocean and Delaware Bay. It has a large harbor and is one of the primary headquarters for the U.S. Coast Guard. It is a town with a genuine nautical history.

We were staying in one of the bed-and-breakfast places. It was off-season, the weather was terrible and the weather reports were downright frightening. As a result, by the second night we were the only guests in this particular inn.

Usually the people who run bed-and-breakfast places are so busy taking care of their guests they have little time for extended conversations. But this stormy night we sat in the parlor before a cheery fire and chatted about this and that with our host.

He turned out to be quite an interesting fellow. He had been a homicide detective in Philadelphia before retiring to the far gentler career of innkeeper. He asked me the inevitable question:

"And what do *you* do?"

I said I was a writer.

"What do you write about?"

I said that I wrote about lots of things and that I had done quite a number of books on ghosts.

Then he said something which made my ears prick up and my nose twitch. "Did you know this place is haunted?"

"Oh, really." I tried to sound casual, but I was like a hunting dog on the scent. I had just signed a contract to do a book on ghosts of the sea, this book, in fact, and here I was in a seaside town being told that I was staying in a haunted house. "Tell me about it."

The story was a fairly typical one as accounts of hauntings go. There were the ghostly footsteps, the doors that seemed to open and close mysteriously. There was the uncanny feeling of being watched while you were sure you were alone. And there were sightings.

Several guests had described a large man wearing a dark, loose coat that extended halfway between his waist and knees. It sounded like what was called a pea-coat, which was once popular with sailors, particularly merchant seamen. Here, I thought, was my nautical ghost.

There was nothing frightening or threatening about the ghost. A couple of guests thought that he might have been another guest or perhaps a workman who had wandered into their room by accident. No one had felt the need to shorten their stay.

The innkeeper used his training in investigation to try to find out about the ghost. He checked court records and newspaper files to learn more of the background of the house. He was particularly looking for tales of violent death, murder or suicide that might have taken place there. These are the sort of events traditionally believed to trigger a haunting. Nothing sensational turned up. But he did find that before it had been turned into a guest house, for much of its history the building had been owned by people who had either been sailors or had close connections with the sea. A sailor's ghost would not have been out of place.

Then I asked our host the question that I have been asked so often. "Did you see the ghost yourself?"

He said he had, and his story was the most remarkable of all. He had only owned the house for about four years. Shortly after he took it over and before he had heard of ghostly sightings by anyone else, he was having some renovations done, and there were no guests in the house. Since it was Sunday there were no workmen either. In the middle of the afternoon the new innkeeper was working on the front lawn when he spied a large man in a dark coat enter the front door.

No one was supposed to be in the house. The former detective didn't like the idea of strangers wandering around his property. And he knew how to conduct a search. He went into the house and locked all the entrances. Then he went up to the top floor and began to search methodically. After he had searched a room, he carefully locked it. He said he doubted if even a mouse could have escaped detection, let alone a large man. He had clearly seen the man go into the house. He couldn't have gotten out. Yet he wasn't there. Puzzling. The former policeman was sure he hadn't been seeing things. He couldn't explain what he had seen.

The incident was nearly forgotten in all the details of getting ready for his new business, until he began hearing stories of the ghostly presence from some of his guests.

"Where is the ghost usually seen?" I asked.

"Oh, up in the third-floor room, where you and your wife are staying."

What an opportunity! I resolved to stay awake to try and see the spectral sailor. With a storm beating at the windows, it was a perfect night for a ghost.

My wife, who thinks that my interest in this sort of stuff is a lot of nonsense, fell asleep immediately. I recall that she snorted at me derisively when I told her what I planned to do. "You'll never stay awake," she said.

Unfortunately she was right. If the ghost entered my room that night, he didn't make enough noise to wake me up.

The same thing happened the following night. And after that it was time to leave.

"Did you see the ghost?" the innkeeper asked as we were checking out. I was once again in the familiar position of looking down and shuffling my feet and admitting that I had not. I hadn't even heard as much as a ghostly footstep. The spirits had once again eluded me.

But there are plenty of people who have not been as unlucky, or in many cases, as lucky as I was. They have seen their ghostly sailors, and often as not wished they hadn't.

In the pages that follow you will meet some of them.

CHAPTER ONE

The Admiral Returns

In the classic 1949 British film comedy *Kind Hearts and Coronets* there is a scene of a naval disaster. A bone-headed admiral, played by Alec Guinness, orders his ship to turn the wrong way. His junior officers tell him that if he turns that way, he will surely ram another ship and sink. The admiral, stubborn as he is stupid, refuses to change his order. As a result, there is a collision and the ship sinks. The admiral is seen going down with his ship, saluting stiffly. At last all that can be seen is his hat floating on the water.

The film played this for laughs, and it is very funny. But the scene is clearly based on a real and very tragic incident, the worst peacetime naval disaster of the century. The reason for the disaster remains one of the great mysteries of naval history. And the disaster has spawned one of the most famous naval ghost stories.

In 1893 Admiral Sir George Tryon was commander in chief of the British fleet in the Mediterranean. Though the Royal Navy was not actually engaged in any wars at the time, it was the most powerful naval force the world had ever seen. The navy was the symbol of the might of the British Empire, and the mere appearance of a squadron of British ships off the coast of practically any country would be a stern, if unspoken, warning against defying the wishes of the British. British ships would sail around from one nation to another conducting complicated maneuvers off the coast, just to show how good they were. It was a policy known as "showing the flag."

On June 22, 1893, the Mediterranean fleet, consisting of eight battleships, three armored cruisers and two light cruisers, was conducting maneuvers off the coast of Tripoli. Admiral Tryon commanded the fleet from aboard his flagship *Victoria*. He had the ships form up into two parallel columns. The *Victoria* was at the head of one column, while the battleship *Camperdown*, under the command of Rear Admiral Albert Markham, headed the other. Admiral Tryon issued the order to have the two columns of ships reverse direction by turning inward toward one another. This was a standard maneuver and would have been perfectly safe if the two columns of ships had been far enough away from one another. But they weren't. They were so close that turning inward would mean that the *Victoria* and the *Camp-*

erdown would collide, with disastrous results. Collisions of ordinary ships are bad enough, but the *Camperdown*'s bow had been reinforced with a steel ram so that during a battle it could deliberately run into other ships and sink them.

Everyone on both ships knew that the maneuver was going to lead to a deadly collision—everyone, that is, except Admiral Tryon. As the two huge warships were bearing down on one another, he was looking off in the other direction. It is important to know that this did not take place on a fog-shrouded and stormy night. It was the middle of a hot, sunny afternoon, and the sea was dead calm. Nor was this a decision made in the heat of battle. The fleet was ordered to perform a standard maneuver under ideal conditions.

Admiral Tryon was an experienced, knowledgeable and highly respected officer. He was described as a superb technician and a "mastermind." The orders of all British naval officers, and certainly admirals, were law and supposed to be carried out immediately and without question. But particularly in peacetime even the strict regulations allowed for some independence of action when there was reason to believe that an order was utterly insane, as this order clearly was. Tryon himself was held in awe by his subordinates, but he had never been considered an unreasonable man or a despot; he was a man who could be reasoned with.

Aboard the *Camperdown* Rear Admiral Markham hesitated for a moment before carrying out the order to turn. From the *Victoria* came the message, "What are you waiting for?" So he began the maneuver and saw the two ships bearing down on one another. Markham was convinced, almost until the last moment, that Tryon had some plan in mind, that somehow he would change direction or do something to avoid the collision. The other officers aboard the *Victoria* knew that Admiral Tryon had made a terrible error, but they all hoped that someone else would tell him about it. They all fell back on the training that an order was an order and had to be carried out no matter what.

Finally when these two gigantic ships were less than 200 yards from one another, Markham gave the order to reverse direction. At the same time, Tryon also seemed to recognize what was going to happen and gave the same order. It was too late. In fact, the final change of direction made the disaster worse.

At exactly 3:43 P.M. the *Camperdown*'s bow sliced into the *Victoria,* tearing up the deck to a depth of nine feet. If the two ships had remained locked together, the greater tragedy might have been avoided. But by this time the *Camperdown* was already going backwards. As she pulled slowly out of the wedge-shaped tear, the water poured in.

The accident had taken place only four miles from shore, and at first Tryon appeared to believe that he could steam toward the shore and would be able to beach the *Victoria* before she sank. But the damage was too great. Within five minutes the ship had begun to go down.

There was no panic among the officers or the perfectly trained crew. They tried to get to their lifeboats in good order, but there wasn't the time. In the end, some 355 of the 600 aboard the *Victoria* died.

Throughout the last terrible minutes Admiral Tryon remained on the ship's bridge. He was completely calm, and he never told anyone what he had intended when he ordered the ships to turn toward one another. All he was heard to say—to no one in particular—was, "It's all my fault—entirely my fault."

In the best naval tradition Admiral Sir George Tryon went down with his ship.

When news of the disaster reached Britain, it created a sensation. The flagship of the proud Mediterranean fleet had been accidentally sunk by another British warship in broad daylight! Why? An explanation was needed. There were public investigations and inquiries, but no satisfactory explanation was ever offered.

The subject of the sinking of the *Victoria* has been reexamined by naval historians countless times. Every scrap of information that we know, or are ever likely to know, has been looked at from every angle. But the only witness who could ever really answer the crucial question, Admiral Tryon himself, was dead. So we will probably never know any more than we do now.

There are lots of theories. One is that Tryon had been testing the ability of his officers to make their own decisions. If that is the case the test failed.

The most probable reason is that the admiral was just

not paying attention and made a fatal mistake. He was very experienced and competent, the error he made was obvious and he had plenty of time to detect and correct it. Yet he didn't. There seems to be a missing piece somewhere.

That's the mystery. Now here's the ghost.

On the evening of June 22, 1893, Lady Tryon, the admiral's wife (widow, actually, though she didn't know it at the time), was giving a big reception at the couple's luxurious home in London's Eaton Square. A large, heavyset man wearing an admiral's full uniform came down the stairs to greet the guests, many of whom he knew by name. All of the guests knew him; he was Admiral Tryon.

Lady Tryon never saw the man. She was puzzled at first and then annoyed by the stream of people who came up to her and said how nice it was that the admiral was able to get away from his duties to attend the reception. "What a surprise it is to see Sir George again, Lady Tryon. How did you get him away from his ships to attend the reception?"

She kept repeating to people that Sir George could not possibly be at the reception because he was in command of the fleet in the Mediterranean. In fact, at that moment his body lay at the *bottom* of the Mediterranean.

It was not until she was having breakfast the following morning that she received the fatal news of the sinking of the *Victoria* and her husband's death. In 1893 the world did not possess the sort of instant communication that we have today. There was the telegraph, but still it took many hours for the news of the disaster to reach London. There was no way that the guests at the reception could have known what had happened half a world away.

Did people actually see the ghost of Admiral Sir George Tryon? There is, of course, no way of knowing. But in ghostly lore one of the most common types of reported events is called, by people who investigate such things, a "crisis apparition." It is where the figure of a person who has just died or is facing some sort of life-threatening crisis is seen by friends or loved ones hundreds or even thousands of miles away. This sort of experience has been reported countless times.

So there you have it: a double mystery, two unknowns for the price of one.

CHAPTER TWO

The Sleeping Sailor

In the early years of the nineteenth century, Portsmouth, England, was one of the busiest seaports in the world. One day a well-to-do merchant named Hamilton came to Portsmouth as he had many times before. He was to board a ship there the following day, which was to take him abroad on a business trip.

Hamilton had never cared for Portsmouth, with its crowd of drunken sailors and exotic travelers. As his carriage rolled through the streets, he noticed that the town seemed to be exceptionally crowded and noisy, and not just with sailors and travelers. There was a large number of country people milling about. This made Portsmouth even less attractive to Hamilton, who hated crowds. But he thought, "Business is business, and I'll only be here one night."

Hamilton went directly to the inn where he usually stayed when he was in the port city, and that is where he received his first shock. When he asked for a room, he was informed there was none available. The landlord told him that he had even rented the loft over the stable.

"Well, where can I find a place to spend the night?" said the irritated Hamilton.

The landlord was not very encouraging. He said that not only was there an exceptionally large number of ships in port at the time, but there was also a local election, and people had come in from the outlying districts to vote. That's why all the country people were in town. The landlord doubted that there would be any rooms available in Portsmouth, and he suggested that Hamilton travel to some nearby town to find accommodations.

This was not a suggestion that the merchant liked at all. He had a great deal of faith in himself and his money and was sure that he would be able to rent a room someplace, even if he had to pay extra.

But as Hamilton went about Portsmouth, he became more and more discouraged. He tried inns that he would never have considered on earlier occasions and found them fully occupied. He was told that there were people sleeping in halls and on tables. Not even the offer of extra money seemed able to pry a room loose.

Finally toward evening the merchant was feeling

tired, hungry and not a little desperate. Would he have to sleep in the gutter like a beggar? He found himself in an unfamiliar part of the city. There on a quiet sidestreet he found an inn called The Admiral Collingwood. A sign over the door contained a poorly painted likeness of the admiral.

It was not the sort of place that Hamilton was used to, but it looked fairly clean and as noted he was feeling desperate. The landlady of The Admiral Collingwood told Hamilton that there was an empty room. But she added that the room had a large bed in it and was usually rented to two people. She asked him if he would mind sharing.

This was not a prospect that Hamilton cared for in the least. He said that since no one had rented the room yet, he would be willing to pay double for it if he could have it to himself.

The landlady shrugged. If the gentleman wished to throw his money away in that fashion, it was fine with her.

Hamilton went up to look at the room. It was fairly shabby, but clean. There were a few pieces of unattractive furniture scattered about, and it contained an enormous bed. All in all it wasn't too bad; he had expected much worse. Feeling greatly relieved and rather pleased with himself, the merchant went downstairs and ordered an enormous dinner. He was extremely hungry for he had not eaten anything while he had searched for a place to stay.

The meal and a few glasses of wine made him drowsy, and he headed upstairs to bed. He intended to get up early the next morning and go down to the docks to board his ship. Before retiring, he looked out of the window of his room. There wasn't a lot to see, just the backs of a few houses and a small plot of land behind the inn. He noticed that some of the ground appeared to have been dug up recently, and he wondered if someone was going to plant a garden.

It's a bit late in the year to start a garden, he thought. But he didn't worry much about it. He carefully locked the door to his room. The Admiral Collingwood was unfamiliar to him, and one always had to be on the lookout for thieves.

Hamilton then undressed, slipped under the covers and was soon asleep. Something, perhaps it was a noise, woke him. The moonlight was streaming through the window. He looked at his watch, which he had hung on a chair beside the bed. He had been asleep for less than two hours. He muttered to himself and then turned over and prepared to go back to sleep. But the moment he turned over, he nearly jumped out, for he found himself face to face with another occupant of the bed.

In the moonlight Hamilton was able to make out the figure of the other fellow. He was a muscular young man, shirtless, but wearing the type of bell-bottomed trousers favored by sailors. He had what appeared to be a red kerchief wrapped around his head. His most prominent feature was the magnificent dark sidewhiskers that he wore. The figure lay half-propped up on top of the covers and appeared to be deeply asleep.

From alarm, Hamilton's reaction quickly shifted to anger. He had paid double for this room so that he could be alone. That thieving landlady must have rented it to someone else anyway. He would wake the intruder up and throw him out.

But as Hamilton stared at the other man, he thought better of that bold plan. The fellow was much younger and stronger than he was. He was a sailor and probably drunk, and these drunken sailors had a reputation for violence. No, he thought, I won't wake him up. I'll just let him sleep it off. He's not making any noise. He's not even snoring. I'll just go back to sleep myself. This is, after all, a very big bed. In the morning I'll give that landlady a piece of my mind.

Satisfied with his plan, the merchant rolled over and went back to sleep. As he drifted off, a disturbing thought passed through his mind. He had securely locked the door from the inside. How had the sailor managed to get past the locked door? But Hamilton was very tired, and the thought didn't trouble him for long. He was soon asleep again.

When Hamilton opened his eyes in the morning, he found that the bewhiskered young sailor was still there. He did not seem to have moved at all during the night. The light was better now, and he was able to see the young man more clearly. What he saw was unsettling.

What in the moonlight had looked like a red bandanna, he now saw was a rag that had been soaked in blood. The sailor himself looked pale and ill. This man was not sleeping; he looked unconscious.

Hamilton dressed quickly and prepared to leave the room. As he did, he realized that the room door was still locked from the inside, and the key was in his pocket. The landlady must have given him a second key, Hamilton thought. I don't know how he was able to use a key in his condition.

Downstairs Hamilton confronted the landlady. "I suppose you expect me to pay for my room," he said.

"Of course, sir. Double the usual rate, as you promised."

"Well, I'm not going to pay double. I'm not going to pay anything. You can collect your money from the other fellow."

"Other fellow? I'm sure I don't know what you're talking about, sir."

The landlady looked puzzled and innocent, and Hamilton thought, She's a good liar. Probably has had lots of practice. Controlling his temper as best he could, the merchant went on to explain that there was a strange man in the room he had rented.

"That's impossible, sir. No one came in after you did last evening. You have the only key to the room, and before I went to bed I bolted the front door."

"Well, I don't know how he got there," stormed the merchant, "but he's still there. Come, I'll show you."

He led the woman upstairs, threw open the door to his room and pointed at the bed. "There!" he said triumphantly. But the bed was empty.

"I don't understand," said the merchant. "He was completely unconscious when I left him. He had been injured. There was a bloody rag tied around his head."

Suddenly all the color drained from the landlady's face. "Was he a young man, with great dark sidewhiskers?"

"Yes, that was the fellow."

The landlady began to weep. "He's come back. Now everyone will know, and I'll be ruined."

The woman, who was very near hysteria, began to explain. A few days earlier a group of sailors who had been drinking had come to the inn. Though they were clearly drunk, they didn't seem troublesome, and the landlady served them some more drinks. Then quite suddenly an argument flared up, and one of the sailors, a young man with dark sidewhiskers, was struck in the head. He fell to the floor, unconscious and bleeding. The other sailors ran out and disappeared into the darkness. The landlady and her servants did what they could. They bound up his wound with strips torn from his shirt. They then carried him upstairs to a room—Hamilton's room—and laid him on the bed. But by this time he was already dead.

If she called the authorities, then everyone would know that a murder had taken place in her establishment. That would not be good for business, and business wasn't very good anyway. This news might ruin her.

She hit on a plan. The only people who knew what had happened were the other sailors and her servants. The sailors wouldn't tell anyone because they had been involved in the killing, and her servants wouldn't talk because if they did, they would be out in the street. The body could be taken down to the back garden and buried there. (Hamilton recalled the patch of newly disturbed earth he had seen from his window.) Sailors disappeared all the time. This one would never be missed. And no one need ever know what had happened.

"But now he's come back. People will say the place is haunted, and I'll be ruined."

Hamilton was sure of only one thing—he didn't want to get involved. All he wanted to do was get out of The Admiral Collingwood as quickly as possible, board his ship and leave Portsmouth forever. He reassured the landlady that he would tell no one what he had seen and heard. He paid her double, as he had promised, and ran out of the door. As he left, he could hear the landlady shouting, "Bless you, sir. Bless you."

Hamilton managed to avoid Portsmouth for sixteen years. But then business required that he return to the city. His initial horror at his experience had softened over time and was replaced by curiosity. He made his way back to the street where The Admiral Collingwood had been located. It wasn't there anymore. The building which once held the inn had been converted into a grocer's shop.

Hamilton asked the grocer about the inn. The grocer didn't know very much. He said that the inn had closed many years ago, and the building had remained vacant until he bought it at a very good price. The grocer said he had no idea why the inn had closed.

Hamilton shuddered. He knew why.

CHAPTER THREE

The Actor's Voice

During the 1930s and 1940s, one of the most popular leading men in Hollywood was the handsome actor Tyrone Power. That name, however, would have been familiar to theatergoers both in England and America during the nineteenth century as well. Tyrone Power came from an English acting family, and several other members of the family who had been stars in their own day had the same name. One of them played a part in a great and mysterious tragedy at sea.

In mid-March 1841 there was a tremendous storm in the North Atlantic. The winds and rain reached as far as England. On the night of March 12, 1841, the rain was battering London. In the Blackheath section of the city lived Benjamin Webster, director of the Haymarket Theater and a close friend of the actor Tyrone Power.

As the violence of the storm increased, the noise of rattling doors and windows awakened Webster's butler. The butler thought that the noises were more than just the wind. He was sure he heard someone banging at the front door. And then there was a voice, a person outside calling for Webster and crying out over and over again that he was "drowned in the rain." What is more, the butler was sure that he could recognize it as that of Tyrone Power, who had a very powerful and distinctive voice that the butler had heard many times.

The butler immediately went to Webster's room, and together they went to the front door. But when the door was unbolted and thrown open, no one was there. Nor did there seem to be anyone in the street. Webster was annoyed at having been awakened and was sure his servant had been fooled by the sounds of the storm or had simply dreamed that he heard the voice. The butler respectfully but most definitely disagreed.

Webster, on the other hand, was quite sure that his friend could not have been standing in the rain at his front door because he knew that Tyrone Power was on tour in America. He went back to bed and thought no more about it for the moment.

Webster, however, had only been partially correct. Tyrone Power had been on tour in America, but his tour had ended and he had booked passage back to England on the steam-packet the *President*.

The *President* was one of the early steamships to make a regular crossing of the Atlantic. She had been launched in 1839, and by 1841 had made three successful and very rapid transatlantic crossings. Still there were fears about how well the ship would hold up in a storm. Reportedly even her own captain had referred to her as "a coffin ship." Knowledgeable seafaring men feared that she was unstable and would flounder and perhaps sink in a gale. The ship's owners naturally insisted that she was the most seaworthy vessel afloat.

When the *President* set sail from New York bound for Liverpool, England, on March 11, 1841, the sky was gray, and it looked as if a storm was brewing. But in those days there was no way of predicting how severe a storm might be, and if ships did not sail every time the weather looked threatening, then the entire shipping industry would have been disrupted. The most celebrated passenger on the voyage was Mr. Tyrone Power, who had just completed a hugely successful tour of the larger American cities and had, in addition, made a great deal of money on a land speculation in Texas.

After the *President* steamed out of the harbor and past the Battery, she was never heard from again. Reports of the severe ocean storm began filtering back to New York and England, but many other ships had been at sea in the storm area at the time, and all of them made it back to port successfully. All, that is, except the *President*.

At first when the ship failed to arrive in Liverpool as expected, there was no undue alarm. In the days of the sailing ship, ships were routinely days or even weeks overdue. With the advent of steamships like the *President,* that began to change. The average time for a transatlantic crossing was cut down to about two weeks. Since steamships were less affected by the weather than sailing vessels, long delays were not expected. Still these early steamships were not able to keep to tight schedules, particularly when they faced storms, and there were no radios with which ships could communicate.

On April 2 and 3 a couple of steam-packets that had left New York at about the same time as the *President* did arrive in England. The captains described the crossing as unpleasant and difficult, but not necessarily dangerous. They were surprised to hear that the *President* was missing. They had expected her to arrive at Liverpool long before they did.

Then the rumors began. The *President* was sighted off the coast of Ireland or in the English Channel. Another report put her off Halifax, Nova Scotia, and still another insisted that she had pulled into the port of New Bedford in Massachusetts for repairs or that she had somehow wound up in the West Indies. According to one "reliable" report she was "lying off Liverpool, her masts gone and taking in water." Tyrone Power's wife received a letter, presumably from the actor, saying that the *President* had been damaged and was being repaired at Madeira in Portugal. The letter was a cruel hoax, but it made headlines in England. A bottle was picked up off the Irish coast with a note in it. The note read, "The

President is sinking. May God help us! Tyrone Power."
It was another hoax. No other ship in history had been
reported in so many different places at the same time.

A variety of "experts" sent letters to the newspapers
explaining in great and technical detail how a ship of
that size could not possibly have been lost in the storm
where so many others had survived. The writers speculated on the various places the *President* could be and
assured the public that she would be heard from very
soon. The experts were all wrong. The *President* was
never heard from again.

When the fact that the *President* was lost finally took
hold, many of the same experts who said that she could
never be sunk weighed in to explain what had caused
her sinking. All sorts of explanations were offered, from
poor design to collision with an iceberg or derelict. In
truth, no one knows and no one will ever know. As far
as the rest of the world was concerned, she simply disappeared.

Benjamin Webster learned that his actor friend had
been aboard the missing ship. And his mind turned once
again to the events of the night of March 12. That might
have been the very time when the ship went down. He
became convinced that the spirit of his friend had tried
to reach him at the moment of his death.

Webster had no desire to gain any publicity from this
incident. He shared the facts and his belief with his
family and members of the Power family, but it was not
made public until many years after Webster's own
death.

CHAPTER FOUR

"Pay What I Owe"

Around 1870 a British schoolmaster named William
Bottrell began collecting and publishing stories and legends from his native district of Cornwall in the south-
west of England. He was afraid that many of the old
tales would be forgotten and disappear completely.
There were tales of magic and giants, of demons and
ghosts—lots of stories of ghosts. Since Cornwall has a
long seacoast, many of the stories he collected were
about ghosts of the sea. And for one of these stories
Bottrell did not have to go very far, because it was about
one of his own relatives.

As a young man James Bottrell had been a privateer—
that was sort of a legal pirate. The British government

allowed privateers to attack and plunder the ships of Britain's enemies, so long as they gave a percentage of the spoils back to the government. In 1850, after spending many years as a privateer, James bought himself a farm near the Cornish town of Zennor and settled down to a quieter and much safer life on land.

One stormy winter evening James was roused from a sound sleep by the sound of knocking on his bedroom window. He looked out and thought he saw the face of his old shipmate and friend John Jones, looking very pale and sad, staring in at him through the window. The face then disappeared, and James convinced himself he had been dreaming. As far as he knew, John Jones was still alive.

But if it was a dream, it turned out be a recurring one, for the same apparition appeared at the window every night for a week, and each time it seemed to stay longer. His house began to be afflicted by strange and unexplainable noises, day and night.

After a week matters became much worse. The ghost began following James around during the day. Its looks, which had first been sad, had grown progressively angrier. James' friends could not see the ghost, but they believed in ghosts, as did most of the people of Cornwall in those days, and they took the matter very seriously indeed. His friends told him that he should try to speak to it, particularly since it was the ghost of an old friend. They said that the spirit would never speak until spoken to and that the ghost probably wanted James to perform some duty it could not. They also warned that it was dangerous to delay in speaking to such a ghost.

So James Bottrell gathered up all his courage, and one day, while walking through a field with the ghost close behind, he turned and said, "Tell me, John Jones, what do you want?"

The ghost, which had been looking very angry, suddenly smiled. "It is good that you have spoken, for I would have been the death of you if you had delayed much longer. I was angry because my old friend seemed to reject and fear me."

"I don't fear you any longer, Jack. What is it that you want me to do?"

The ghost of John Jones explained that the night before he had first appeared, he had accidentally fallen overboard during a storm while serving on a ship in the Bay of Biscay. As he was drowning, he thought of his old friend James Bottrell. He said that he had left a chest containing a good deal of money at an inn in Plymouth. It was an inn they had often stayed at together when they were shipmates. He wanted James to go to Plymouth, get the chest and use the money to pay off his debts. "Keep what remains for yourself. I'll meet you in Plymouth and tell you exactly what to do."

The next morning James Bottrell rode off to Plymouth and took a room at an inn near the one where the chest had been left.

As he lay in his bed trying to figure out what he was going to tell the landlady so that she would give him the chest, the ghost appeared again. "Don't think that the landlady will make any difficulty about taking away the chest, for she doesn't know it contains valuables or that I am dead. She knows we were good friends. Tell her I'm in town and will see her before I leave. Tomorrow bring the chest here, and I'll tell you how to deal with my creditors."

The landlady was very glad to see James and quite relieved to have the sailor's chest taken off her hands. She said that she would be glad to see Captain Jones (as she called him) and that he should be sure to visit her before he left port again.

When James opened the chest, he could see nothing but seaman's clothing. But the ghost showed him that the money was concealed beneath a false bottom. The ghost then directed him around to all the shops where it had outstanding bills and made sure that every debt was paid in full. Then the ghost disappeared, but without saying good-bye.

James walked down to the dock and was looking over the water when the ghost suddenly appeared next to him. He looked younger and fitter than he had before and was dressed in all new clothes. "I've just passed by the old inn," he said, "showed myself as I now appear and blew a kiss to our old hostess, who was at her work near an open window; but, before she could reach her door to welcome home the man she used to admire, lo! I'm here. So you see, it's convenient to be a ghost!"

The ghost then told James he was "off to sea again."

"You will not see me again while you are alive, but if you think of me at the hour of your death we shall meet again. My poor body lies deep in the Bay of Biscay, and when yours is laid in the Zennor churchyard we will rove the sea together."

A fine ship had pulled up at the dock, though no one but James and the ghost seemed to be aware of it. The ghost bid James a final farewell and disappeared aboard the ship. The ship itself seemed to glide toward the horizon with amazing speed, until it too vanished. James Bottrell stood for a long time looking out at the empty ocean.

As James returned home, he felt pretty pleased with himself. He had helped his dead friend pay off his debts and in return had received some fine clothes and a considerable sum of money. It was not what most people expect when they encounter a ghost.

CHAPTER FIVE

The Wrecker, the Curse and the Bell

William Bottrell's account of his own ancestor's experience with a ghost is quite cheerful, for a ghost story. But not all of the tales he collected from his native Cornwall were so sunny; some were grim and terrible indeed.

"More than a hundred years ago," wrote Bottrell, "a dark strange man appeared in St. Just; no one knew whence he came, but it was supposed that he was put ashore from a pirate ship by way of marooning him."

The stranger seemed to have plenty of money. He rented an isolated farmhouse near the shore. After a while people began to wonder why so many ships seemed to be wrecked on the cliffs that bordered the stranger's farm. The reason was that the stranger was the most terrible of nautical criminals, a wrecker. On dark and stormy nights he would fasten a lantern to a horse's neck and then drive the horse along the cliff near his house. The bobbing motion of the lantern looked like a light from a vessel.

Those aboard ships sailing by would think that there was plenty of sea room. They would come in too close to the shore and be broken up by the rocks. Anyone who happened to survive the wreck would be killed by the wrecker, so there would be no witnesses. The wrecker would then loot the remains of the ship.

Says Bottrell, "He lived long and became rich by his sin." But in the end there was the Devil to pay. As the evil old man lay dying, he began screaming, "Do save me from the Devil, and the sailors there, looking to tear me to pieces."

Several parsons were sent for to drive the Devil out of the wrecker's house. But nothing worked. Though the house was a good bit inland, the dying man's room was filled with the sound of the pounding sea.

A couple of farmhands working a field overlooking the sea heard a hollow voice coming from the water: "The hour is come, but the man is not come."

Looking out over the waves, they saw a black, heavy, square-rigged ship with all its sails set coming in fast against the wind and tide. No one could be seen aboard the ship. Then a black cloud rose and seemed to gather around the dying wrecker's house. There were sounds of thunder, and the black cloud rolled off toward the death ship, which sailed away at once amid a blaze of lightning. It soon disappeared over the horizon.

The weather cleared suddenly, and when people fearfully entered the wrecker's chamber they found him dead. The plan was to bury him as quickly as possible. At the funeral those who carried the coffin swore that it was too light to contain a body. Once again the sky suddenly became dark, and it began to rain. The storm was so severe that the pallbearers dropped the coffin and rushed into the church for safety.

When the storm was over, they ventured out. There was nothing left of the coffin but its handles and a few nails, for it had been struck by lightning.

On the evening of October 22, 1707, a fleet of ships led by the flagship the *Association*, commanded by Admiral Sir Cloudsley Shovell, struck the rocks about three and one half miles from the little town of St. Agnes. It was a terrible tragedy. The ships all went down in a few moments, and those aboard perished, except one man who was able to save himself by clinging to a piece of floating timber. When the weather cleared, he was plucked from a rock in the sea, a few miles from where the *Association* went down.

The survivor had a strange tale to tell. He said that the day before the admiral's ship was wrecked, one of the crew, a Cornwall native who was well-acquainted with the area in which the *Association* and the rest of the fleet were sailing, told the admiral that the course they were on would take them too close to the dangerous rocks. The admiral and his officers were incensed that an ordinary seaman would question their judgment. But the sailor persisted in saying that the ships were on a course that would lead them to destruction. The admiral's response was to order the man condemned to be hanged for insubordination and attempting to incite a mutiny.

Just before the poor fellow was about to be hanged, he requested that a psalm from the Bible be read. It was not a request that could be refused. Then the condemned man chose the 109th Psalm.

Among the people of Cornwall the 109th Psalm is known as "the cursing psalm" and is very much feared. It contains lines like this:

"When he shall be judged, let him be condemned: and let his prayer become sin.

"Let his days be few; and let another take his office.

"Let his children be fatherless, and his wife a widow."

The request terrified many of the sailors aboard the *Association,* but there was no way for Sir Cloudsley to withdraw permission for a reading from the Bible. The condemned man's last words were that Sir Cloudsley Shovell and those who saw him hanged should never reach the land alive.

The hanged man's body was wrapped in canvas and cast into the sea. A short time later the storm that had been threatening all day broke. The fear among the crew increased when the dead man's corpse, stripped of its canvas covering, was seen bobbing on the waves near the ship and floating toward her. The corpse continued to follow the *Association* until she struck the rocks, when the hanged man disappeared beneath the water with the ship that he had cursed. Several other ships in the admiral's fleet were also wrecked during the storm. In all, about 2,000 officers and men perished in the disaster.

The admiral's body washed ashore in the bay near St. Mary's, and he was buried in the sand. Tradition holds that a pit still marks his grave and that the pit never fills with water even during the greatest storms. Supposedly nothing ever grows there, though the ground around it is always green.

In the churchyard of St. Levan's there is the grave of one Captain Wetherel. He was drowned when his ship sank off the Cornish coast shortly before midnight. The captain ordered his crew to the lifeboats, but refused to leave the ship himself. As the ship was sinking, the crew heard the captain give eight loud and distinct strokes on the bell—eight bells—the sailor's signal for midnight.

His body was recovered and was buried in St. Levan's churchyard. Almost immediately the rumor sprang up that anyone passing the churchyard at midnight would hear the ghostly sound of eight bells coming from Captain Wetherel's grave.

One day a young seaman heard the story and boldly declared that it was all a lot of nonsense. In order to prove it, he went to the churchyard at midnight determined to stand near the captain's grave. His friends remained behind. A short while later the young man returned looking pale and shaken. He said to his friends, "True as I'm alive, I heard eight bells struck in the grave and wouldn't go near the spot again for the world."

On his next voyage the young sailor was lost at sea.

Since that time no one would purposely go to the graveyard to hear the captain's bell. The general belief was that bad luck, or even death, would soon overtake anyone who did hear the ghostly bell.

CHAPTER SIX

Faces in the Water

One of the great frustrations for those of us who collect ghostly lore is the lack of physical evidence. Stories are all very well and good. When they are well documented and come from credible witnesses, they can even be extremely impressive and believable. But in the end a story is a story. It depends on the memory and the honesty of the witness. What we really want is hard evidence, something we can touch or look at—something like a photograph.

In the century and a half since photography became popular, there have been lots of "ghost pictures." Most of these are obvious fakes or the result of an accidental double exposure or some other sort of photographic error. A few remain genuinely mysterious and puzzling. One of the best comes from the sea.

Here is the story:

On December 1, 1929, the oil tanker *Waterton,* owned by the Cities Service Corporation, was bound from California to Panama. It was to go through the Panama Canal and on to the port of New Orleans. Two of the crewmen, James Courtney and Michael Meehan, were engaged in the dirty and dangerous job of cleaning one of the tanks of the giant ship. Something—no one is really sure what—went wrong, and the two men were overcome by the fumes of the cleaning materials and died.

The next day they were buried at sea. Their wrapped and weighted bodies were dropped into the water and sank immediately. It was a sad occasion for the crew of the *Waterton,* for Courtney and Meehan had been quite popular with their shipmates.

The day following the burial one of the ship's officers was scanning the sea when he saw something unusual. It appeared to be two faces bobbing up and down in the waves near the *Waterton.* Though he could not be absolutely sure, they appeared to be the faces of the two men who had just been buried. Moreover, the images seemed to be keeping pace with the ship. Others aboard saw the faces as well, but when the ship was slowed to try to get closer to the apparitions, they faded and disappeared. A few minutes later they would reappear a little farther from the *Waterton.* It was as if the faces were trying to keep a distance from the ship, yet stay in view.

For the following two days the faces reappeared. As before, they kept about forty feet from the ship. Though sailors are notorious for being superstitious, there was no fear or even undue alarm on the *Waterton* over the ghostly faces. They clearly meant no harm. In fact, when the ship later ran into a storm, some men aboard speculated that their dead shipmates were trying to warn them.

There was, of course, a great deal of curiosity. Today it is probable that half the men aboard would have cameras and try to take photographs of the faces in the water. But cameras were not nearly as common or as easy to use in 1929. There wasn't a single camera aboard the *Waterton* on this trip.

The end of the voyage for the *Waterton* was the port of New Orleans. The captain of the ship reported the puzzling incident to his employers, who were very intrigued. On the off-chance that the ghostly faces might reappear on the return voyage, the captain was provided with a camera and film. He was told to try to get a picture of the phenomenon.

Nothing unusual happened on the return voyage until the ship had passed through the Panama Canal and was again in the Pacific in the vicinity of where Courtney and Meehan had been killed. Then one evening the faces appeared again. By the next morning they were close enough to the ship, and there was enough light for the captain to use his camera. He snapped a full roll of film—eight pictures.

A few hours after the photos were taken, the faces

disappeared and did not reappear for the remainder of the voyage.

When the *Waterton* docked in California, the captain took his undeveloped film to the company offices. They arranged to have it processed immediately. Anxious executives examined the negatives while they were still wet. The first seven showed nothing but a grainy picture of the empty ocean. But on the eighth negative there appeared the faint image of two faces in the water.

The story and the picture were printed in the Cities' Service Corporation magazine. Friends and relatives of James Courtney and Michael Meehan positively identified the faces as those of the two dead men.

The faces never reappeared on any future voyage of the *Waterton*.

The picture itself remains one of the most puzzling in the entire history of ghostly lore.

CHAPTER SEVEN

The Great Eastern

In the middle of the nineteenth century, shipping in the world was just beginning to change over from sail to steam. The iron-hull steamships that made the transatlantic voyages were still relatively small and slow. While steamships were clearly the wave of the future, shipbuilders were very cautious about rapidly increasing the size of the ships they built.

A man named Isambard Kingdom Brunel thought they were too cautious. Brunel, a successful builder of bridges and railroads, was confident that it was technically possible to build a really large steamship. He also knew that the larger the ship, the larger the profit it could make on every voyage. His idea was not only to build the largest steamship in the world, but to build one that was five times larger than any other steamship of his day. It was to be the length of two football fields.

His ship was called *The Great Eastern,* and he had planned that it would run from London to Australia and carry most of the world's freight and passenger traffic on that long haul.

Brunel managed to sell his vision to a large number of investors, and construction on the monster ship began in London's best shipyard. The most revolutionary feature of Brunel's *Great Eastern* was to be its double hull, two iron skins three feet apart. It was literally a ship within a ship, with a sealed compartment separating the two. The outer skin could be gashed, but the great ship would remain afloat.

The other statistics for *The Great Eastern* were mind-boggling for that time. There were to be ten huge boilers, fed by 112 furnaces. The smoke would be carried away by five enormous funnels, or smokestacks. The boilers would generate the power to turn two fifty-eight-foot paddle wheels and a twenty-four-foot propeller. Just in case there was a power failure, Brunel's giant ship had six towering masts and an enormous expanse of sail. She would also carry ten anchors weighing five tons each. Brunel believed that he had thought of everything.

This was to be no stripped-down cargo ship, but a luxury liner whose interior would match that of the most fashionable hotels in the world. There were carved walnut seats covered in velvet cushions, paneling and cut-glass mirrors, even "artificial moonlight" provided by gaslight.

Because no ship of this size had ever been built before, the builders faced some unique technical problems. One of the most difficult was that it could not be launched in the ordinary way. Normally ships built in this yard were launched stern first into the river Thames. *The Great Eastern,* however, was due to be launched sideways. It was to be pushed into the water by two specially designed hydraulic rams.

During the last stages of the construction one of the workmen, a master shipwright, disappeared. He had been working on the double hull, and a rumor spread that he had been accidentally sealed up inside it. But most did not take the rumor seriously. Workmen occasionally walked off the job for personal reasons. The rumor was certainly not going to spoil the immense vessel's debut.

The great ship was due to be launched on November 2, 1857. Everything seemed to be ready. The weather was unusually cold and wet, but a large crowd still gathered on the banks of the Thames. Shortly before the scheduled launch a strange hammering sound was heard inside *The Great Eastern.* No one knew where it came from, and it was soon forgotten in the excitement of the moment.

The launch was set in motion, right on schedule. The immense ship moved a couple of feet and stopped. She had become jammed at an awkward angle. Brunel went into conference with the shipbuilders. No one seemed to know what to do. They decided that the only thing they could do was wait until the high water and try again. The crowd began to drift away, and the mysterious hammer blows were heard once more, this time louder than before.

Hours passed, the water rose and the launching was tried again, but with no more success than the first time. Over the next few weeks further attempts were made to launch the immense vessel. During one attempt the hydraulic rams burst. By the end of November it began to look as if *The Great Eastern* would never be launched. One of those who had invested in the project suggested that the ship be left where it was and turned into some sort of amusement pavilion. The more superstitious sailors began to say that the ship was jinxed and that it would be an evil day if the ship ever did go to sea.

Throughout the winter Brunel tried to ease the ship into the water in a variety of ways—nothing worked. Finally, however, nature succeeded where man had failed. By mid-March, spring tides and heavy rains allowed the ship to drift gently into the river. But the delay had cost so much money that Brunel's company went bankrupt, and the ship passed into the hands of new owners.

It wasn't until September 15, 1859, that *The Great Eastern* finally headed downriver and into the open sea. Brunel was not there to witness the event. He had died a few weeks earlier. On the day of Brunel's death the ship's engineer complained that he had been "rudely disturbed by constant hammering from below."

The ship steamed out into bad weather. While other ships had to pull into harbor, the giant steamship seemed to handle the weather with ease. The pilot wrote, "I can state without any hesitation that, with sufficient sea room she is even more easily handled and under command than any ordinary ship, either under sail or steam."

A few minutes later the casing of one of the smokestacks exploded. Six members of the engine-room crew were killed, and the elegant grand ballroom was wrecked.

It was months before she could be repaired. The new owners had given up on the idea of an Australian route. She was to sail to New York on June 17, 1860. But by this time the reputation of *The Great Eastern* was so bad that she carried only thirty-six fare-paying passengers. However, the giant ship made the crossing in a record-breaking eleven days. And it was an entirely uneventful trip.

Her second crossing took only ten days, and this time there were 100 passengers. The third voyage was even more successful, and it began to look as if all the rumors about the ship being evil or jinxed were wrong, or at least that the jinx had been broken.

For the fourth voyage there were over 400 first-class passengers on the great liner. The weather off the Irish coast was bad, but the giant ship barely seemed to notice. Then late in the afternoon the thumping hammer blows were heard once again. Minutes later the ship was hit by a huge wave and nearly capsized. A second wave tore off one of the paddle wheels and washed four of the lifeboats overboard. A barrage of waves followed. The second paddle wheel was shattered, and the rest of the lifeboats disappeared into the raging sea. The luxurious public rooms and cabins were wrecked.

The passengers thought they were going to die and began singing hymns. The crew mutinied and broke into the storeroom where the liquor was kept. The captain gave all the male passengers guns so that they could defend themselves from the drunken sailors.

The big liner drifted helplessly through the night, and by morning the storm subsided. On board the crew recovered from its drunken orgy and set to work trying to patch the ship up as best they could. After two days of work, enough power had been restored to allow *The Great Eastern* to limp back to port. But her days as an ocean liner were over.

The once-luxurious ship was stripped of her furnishings and set to the mundane task of laying cable in the North Atlantic. When that task was finished in 1866, she was put up for sale, but there were no bidders.

For a time her sides were plastered with posters, and she served as sort of a floating billboard. But even that experiment didn't work.

The once mighty *Great Eastern* was an unwanted

derelict for nearly twenty years until she was finally purchased by a company that planned to cut her up and sell the remains as scrap metal. As she was being towed away on her last journey, the lone watchman aboard began hearing the thud of hammer blows. He searched everywhere, but could find no source of the noise on the empty ship. He did remember all the rumors and fears that had once surrounded the ship, and he begged to be taken off. The tugboat crew laughed at his fears, but not one of them offered to replace him aboard the derelict.

As the tugs hauled the wreck away, her lines broke and she nearly was grounded on the coast. It took a tremendous effort to get the giant wreck under control again.

In the yard where *The Great Eastern* was being cut apart, workmen made a gruesome discovery. In the space between the double hull they found a skeleton. Next to the skeleton was a carpetbag of rusted tools, including a hammer. It was the remains of the master shipwright who had been entombed during the final stages of construction.

Was this the source of the hammering sounds and of the bad luck that plagued the great ship? Most of those who worked around the docks of London believed it was. No amount of talk about poor ship design and unfortunate coincidence could convince them otherwise.

And, who knows, maybe they were right.

CHAPTER EIGHT

"Ocean-Born Mary"

There is an old house in the town of Henniker, New Hampshire, that has the reputation of being haunted by the ghost of a tall, red-haired, green-eyed woman.

Now, wait a minute, you say, this is a book about ghosts of the deep, not haunted houses. But the story of this particular haunted house really began at sea. And it's an irresistible tale with a gallant pirate and buried treasure, to boot. The house is known as "Ocean-born Mary's House."

In July 1720 the little sailing vessel *Wolf* was en route from Ireland to America. Aboard were a group of Scotch-Irish emigrants looking for a new and better life. On the morning of July 28, when the ship was just off the Massachusetts coast and very near the end of a difficult journey, Captain James Wilson spotted an unknown ship which he took, quite correctly, to be a pirate ship.

Soon the *Wolf* was boarded by the pirates, who were commanded by a man called Captain Pedro. The outlook for the passengers of the *Wolf* looked grim indeed. As the pirate captain searched the ship, he found a woman clutching a newborn infant. It was the young daughter of Captain Wilson. She had been born at sea to his wife, Elizabeth, just a day or two before the encounter with the pirates.

The sight of the infant had a strange effect on the pirate captain, who began to weep. He said that he would spare the lives of all those aboard the *Wolf* and not take anything from them if Mrs. Wilson would agree to name the baby Mary after his wife. She agreed instantly.

Good as his word, Captain Pedro and his men departed, and all aboard the *Wolf* breathed a sigh of relief. But to their dismay, the pirate captain came back almost immediately. However, it was not to take anything, but to bring a whole armload of valuable presents for the baby. The presents obviously had been stolen from passengers of less fortunate ships. Among the gifts was a large piece of sumptuous greenish-blue brocade silk. Captain Pedro said that this was to be used for Mary's wedding dress.

After delivering his gifts, the pirate sailed off, this time for good.

Many of the passengers of the *Wolf* settled in the town of Londonderry, New Hampshire, where they annually celebrated the day of their deliverance from the pirates. The baby was given the nickname "Ocean-born Mary." And it seems that Captain Pedro regularly sent gifts to his young protégée.

When Mary grew up—and she grew to a height of six feet—she married Thomas Wallace, the only man in town taller than she was. She is described in a history of the town as being "quite tall, resolute, and determined; of strong mind, quick of comprehension, with a strong brogue, and full of humor." She and her family were known as "pillars of the community."

At some point—no one seems quite sure when—Thomas Wallace died, leaving Mary with four sons and a daughter to take care of. And then Captain Pedro once again entered her life.

It seems that the captain decided to give up the pirate's life. He may have been a bit too softhearted to make a really good pirate, anyway. He also thought it wise to settle inland, where he was less likely to be recognized by the authorities or his old pirate compatriots. In his career Captain Pedro had collected a good deal of money, and he bought 100 acres of land in the hilly country several miles from the town of Henniker. He had a large house constructed for himself.

By this time Captain Pedro's wife had either died or had left him. He was quite an old man and needed someone to take care of him. So he contacted Mary to come live with him and be his housekeeper. Mary came to Henniker with her four sons and lived there until she died at the age of ninety-four.

Just how much of the Ocean-born Mary story is truth and how much is legend is difficult to determine. The facts of her birth are well established. What is less certain is whether the man for whom she kept house in Henniker was really Captain Pedro. According to at least one version of the tale, Captain Pedro wasn't really named Pedro; he was, in reality, an Englishman of noble birth who was trying to disguise his true identity by using a Spanish name.

Another part of the story holds that the pirate captain was stabbed to death one night, presumably by a member of his old crew who was searching for the treasure that he had carried away with him.

The treasure is one of the most enduring parts of the Ocean-born Mary tale. Some people believe that Captain Pedro hid the bulk of his treasure someplace around the house where no one has yet been able to locate it, though many have tried. Another part of the legend is that the old pirate's dying wish was to be buried under the hearthstone in the kitchen of the house and that Mary, a dutiful friend, did exactly that. It has also been said that Captain Pedro was buried with his treasure and that anyone who disturbs the hearthstone will die. A man named Tony Eddy was supposed to have died mysteriously after getting permission to dig up the pirate's supposed resting place. After that no one tried.

The ghost of Ocean-born Mary, however, is far from

a malevolent, treasure-guarding spirit. Those who have encountered her have said that she was not only friendly but downright helpful. Gus Roy, who once owned the house, recounted a number of times when the ghost allegedly saved him from death or injury. Once he was about to throw a paper bag into the fire, when he was restrained by an unseen hand. It refused to let him go until he had carefully examined the contents of the bag. He found that it contained blasting powder, and if he had carelessly thrown it into the fire he surely would have been killed. He even said that the ghost had once helped him shore up a garage on the property during a hurricane.

By the 1950s Ocean-born Mary's house appeared in a *Life* magazine article about America's most haunted houses, and it has attracted a lot of attention since. More recent owners of the house have flatly denied that there has been any ghostly activity there at all. But the Ocean-born Mary legend is far too romantic to fade away, and the stories, true or not, will undoubtedly continue to be told.

CHAPTER NINE

The Abandoned Lighthouse

Today the traditional lighthouse is of little importance to sailors. Ships are warned of dangerous shores and rocks by radar and a host of other modern electronic equipment. The lighthouses themselves, those that still exist, now have automatically controlled beacons. The old-fashioned stone lighthouse appears primarily in paintings of the seacoast or is maintained as a picturesque tourist attraction.

But not so very long ago the lighthouse was an absolute necessity for navigation. The lighthouse beacon allowed sailors to fix their location and warned them off dangerous shores and rocks, particularly at night or in bad weather. The lights, often oil lamps, had to be tended with great care and skill. If a light went out, the result could be disaster.

By necessity, lighthouses were usually located in remote and isolated places, and the life of a lighthouse keeper was famous for being lonely. There were no telephones, no televisions and no visitors—just the lighthouse itself and the sea for weeks or months on end. People who for one reason or another decided they wanted to get away from the rest of the human race often said they would become lighthouse keepers.

Despite the loneliness, there is only one well-known case of lighthouse keepers abandoning their post. The place was the Eilean Mor Lighthouse, located on the rocky and otherwise uninhabited Flannan Islands off the west coast of Scotland. This was an exceptionally remote, isolated and stormy spot, even for a lighthouse. And for that reason the beacon from this particular lighthouse was exceptionally important.

On the night of December 15, 1900, the brigantine *Fairwind* was sailing near the Eilean Mor Lighthouse. Two sailors keeping watch on deck saw something in the water that startled and frightened them. A longboat, or what we would more familiarly call a lifeboat, cut directly across their bow, heading toward the lighthouse.

The sailors on the *Fairwind* called out, and though the men in the longboat were close enough to hear, they did not acknowledge the call in any way. The men in the boat wore foul-weather gear, but when the moon shone on their faces they looked pale and ghostly. The sailors' first thought was that they had come across a boatload of floating dead men from some shipwreck. But they could hear the creak of the oarlocks and watch the arms of the rowers moving. The longboat soon disappeared from view.

Later that night a storm broke. It was then that passing ships noticed that the Eilean Mor light was out, and many ships were placed in great danger. Fortunately there were no wrecks because of the absence of the light, but there were plenty of worried and angry skippers.

The first thought was that something had temporarily gone wrong with the light and that it would be fixed shortly. But the days passed, and it did not go on again. There were three men who tended this particular lighthouse, and even if one of them had become ill or died, the others would surely have been able to start the light again or send some sort of distress signal. But the lighthouse remained dark and apparently abandoned.

It wasn't until the day after Christmas that the supply ship *Hesperus* went to the lighthouse to investigate. The *Hesperus* anchored off the shore of the island and signaled the lighthouse repeatedly. There was no answer. A small boat was then sent ashore to investigate. No one came down to the dock to greet them, as was customary when a supply ship arrived.

It was quickly obvious that the lighthouse was empty, but the searchers could find no reason why it should be deserted. There were no signs of violence. There was plenty of food in the larder. Indeed, everything seemed normal and in good order.

As the searchers went through the abandoned structure, they could find only two things that seemed unusual. The men's foul-weather gear, oilskins and seaboots were gone. This seemed to indicate that the three men in the lighthouse had all left at the same time. On the stairs and in the little office where the lighthouse log was kept, there were shreds of seaweed. The searchers, who were experienced sailors and knew all the types of seaweed in the region, could not recognize this particular variety.

That was all that could be found. The absolutely unprecedented disappearance of the three men from the lighthouse was an enormous and ominous mystery. Naturally there was an official inquiry. During the proceedings witness after witness stressed that nothing like this had ever happened before, that no lighthouse keeper had ever abandoned his post, no matter how severe the weather or what the other circumstances might have been. The three men who had run the lighthouse were said to be trustworthy and reliable.

It was hoped that the log book, kept by Thomas Marshall, the head lighthouse keeper, would shed some light on the mystery. His words were read to a hushed courtroom:

"December 12: Gale north by northwest. Sea lashed to fury. Never seen such a storm. Waves very high, Tearing at the lighthouse. Everything shipshape. James

Ducat irritable." An entry made a little later that day read: "Storm still raging, wind steady. Stormbound. Cannot go out. Ship passing, sounding foghorn. Could see lights of cabins. Ducat quiet. Donald McArthur crying."

Marshall's record continued, "December 13: Storm continued through night. Wind shifted west by north. Ducat quiet. McArthur praying." A later entry the same day: "Noon, grey daylight. Me, Ducat and McArthur prayed."

There was no entry for December 14, and for the day the light went out, there was only a single line: "December 15, 1 P.M. Storm ended, sea calm. God is over all."

These entries gave no hint as to what had actually happened to the men, except to indicate that on the days before their disappearance they had been under tremendous emotional strain. What puzzled all who heard what had been written by Thomas Marshall was that the great storm he was describing, on December 12 and 13, had not been noticed by anyone else. On the island of Lewis, a mere twenty miles away, the weather had been unusually calm those days. Had Marshall and his fellow lighthouse keepers, Ducat and McArthur, been suffering from some sort of hallucinations? A fungus that occasionally grows on bread has been known to cause severe hallucinations. It has even been reported to drive men to kill themselves. However, no evidence of this fungus was found at the lighthouse.

What about the unknown longboat with its ghostly

crew of oarsmen that had been sighted by the sailors of the *Fairwind*? And what explanation could there be for the unfamiliar seaweed found in the lighthouse? No explanations were even attempted.

The inquiry itself was concerned only with the hard facts of the case. Local rumors and legends were not allowed as evidence. But there was a strong local belief that the Flannan Islands were haunted. Farmers from nearby islands might keep a flock of sheep on the islands, but they would only check on them during daylight hours. Only fools, like those who kept the lighthouse, dared stay on the islands overnight.

While the board of inquiry could reach no conclusion as to what had happened, the farmers didn't need an explanation. They knew. The islands were haunted by the ghosts of shipwrecked sailors. Sometimes the ghosts came ashore to claim the living.

CHAPTER TEN

The Woman on the Beach

The Bahamas, islands off the southeast coast of the United States, have often been ripped by great storms. In the days of sailing ships there was a tremendous number of wrecks off the shores of these islands, and a shipwreck often results in a ghost story. Great Isaac Cay, a small island of the group, is the scene of one such story.

In 1810, long before a lighthouse had been built on Great Isaac Cay, a hurricane struck the area, and several ships were wrecked. Pieces of ships and bodies of victims washed ashore for days. One of the bodies was that of a woman clutching an infant in her arms. Miraculously the baby was still alive, though barely. The people of the island nursed the child back to health, but what happened to her after that is unknown.

Though the story was widely repeated throughout the islands, there were no ghostly visitations until many years later when workmen began to build a lighthouse on Great Isaac Cay. While walking down the beach one night, a workman saw the hooded figure of a woman coming toward him. Her arms were outstretched, and she was crying, "My baby, my baby!" over and over again. At first the workman wanted to go and help her, but he changed his mind when he saw that the figure was semi-transparent and that he could see the rising moon right through her.

When he recounted the story of his meeting to his fellow workmen, they all laughed at him, but not for long. One by one all the others encountered the same figure on the beach, and though no one had been harmed or threatened by the ghost, they were all heartily glad when the job of building the lighthouse was finished. In August 1859 the lighthouse keeper arrived at the new structure. The departing workmen warned him of what they had seen. He didn't believe them at first. But every time there was a hurricane or a severe storm in the area, the woman was seen walking the beach crying, "My baby, my baby!"

A series of lighthouse keepers were frightened by the specter, but after a while they got used to it. Then, during a storm in 1913, the ghost became bolder. She attempted to climb the spiral staircase of the lighthouse itself. The lighthouse keeper happened to be on his way down the stairs at the time and met the ghost face to face. This threw him into a panic. He raced back up the stairs and slammed the door behind him. He then blocked the door with a heavy crate.

In theory, at least, a ghost should be able to walk right through a door and a crate. But in this case, the ghost didn't. The terrified lighthouse keeper huddled in his room until the sun came up the next morning. Then, ever so carefully, he made his way down the stairs, expecting to meet the ghost at every turn. That very day he applied for a transfer. It was a year before anyone new could be found to take over this particular lighthouse because it had acquired such a bad reputation.

The new lighthouse keeper was a more determined person. It wasn't that he didn't believe in ghosts; he most certainly did. But he also believed that ghosts could be laid to rest if treated properly.

He gathered together a number of the local people and held a solemn funeral service at the spot where the mother and child had been found. This apparently was what the ghost had wanted, for she was never seen on Great Isaac Cay again.

CHAPTER ELEVEN

They Came Back

Submarine warfare was introduced during World War I. These early submarines were primitive compared with the modern submarine. When submerged, they could not communicate with the surface. And when a submarine disappeared, there was usually no way of knowing what had happened to it.

In the year 1919 a British submarine that had been on a routine patrol of the Dutch coast disappeared. The voyage should have taken three weeks, but after eight weeks the sub had not returned or been heard from and was presumed lost. Either she had been detected and sunk by the Germans, or there had been some sort of accident. Accidents were all too common with these early vessels.

The missing sub had been commanded by a fellow called Ryan. That was not his real name; the accounts of the case never gave it because it was felt that the privacy of his family should be protected. He had, however, been quite well known among his fellow submariners and his loss was keenly felt by all who knew him. Ryan was an exceptionally handsome man who always seemed to be cheerful and optimistic despite the dangers that he faced almost daily. He lifted the spirits of anyone he came into contact with. That incessant cheerfulness was a rare and precious quality in the dark and dangerous days of World War I.

When the sub was first reported missing, his friends felt that Ryan, of all people, would somehow pull through. He always had such utter confidence in himself. But after eight weeks that optimistic hope faded, and his friends began to reconcile themselves to the fact of Ryan's death.

Another submarine was sent out to patrol the same area. Because of the danger from German aircraft the sub remained underwater during the day and came to the surface only at night. One sunny morning she was proceeding slowly under the water. Her periscope broke the surface to scan the surrounding area. Suddenly the second officer, who was manning the periscope, cried out, "By Jove! There's old Ryan out there in the water. He's waving to us like mad."

The commander immediately ordered the sub to surface in order to rescue the man in the water. Everyone aboard was tremendously excited at the thought that the popular Ryan had somehow miraculously survived. No one gave a thought to the dangers of surfacing in daylight.

As the sub drew near the spot where Ryan had been sighted, nothing could be seen. He had been spotted only a few minutes earlier. What had happened? Had he sunk beneath the waves? The man sighted through the periscope had not looked like a man who was drowning or indeed in any distress at all. He was smiling cheerfully and waving and seemed to be in perfect control of his situation. Had some sort of mistake been made? The officer who made the sighting was an experienced and levelheaded seaman who had known Ryan well and swore that was the man he saw. He also insisted that he could not be having a hallucination. Ryan had been there, but now he was gone.

If Ryan was no longer visible, there was nothing that could be done. The commander decided there was no point in exposing his vessel and crew to further danger by remaining on the surface. Then something else was sighted in the water just ahead. It was a pair of floating German mines. They lay just in the path that the submarine would have taken. If the submarine had remained below the surface, they would not have been seen until it was too late. The appearance of Ryan, or his ghost, had caused the submarine to change course, and it had saved the lives of the crew.

♦ ♦ ♦

Another return, also from the period of the First World War, was not as pleasant.

The U.S. merchant ship *Monongahela* had an eccentric, one-eyed, red-bearded paymaster. "Pay," as the men called him, loved his whiskey and his ship, in that order. Finally the whiskey caught up with him, and his liver simply gave out.

As he lay dying, he told the sailors who had gathered around to bid him farewell:

"Shipmates, you've been good to me, and I love you for it. I've loved this ship, too, and I can't bear to think of leaving it. I'll come back if I can, and you'll find me in my old cabin, No. 2 on the port side."

Pay's corpse was wrapped in canvas, weighted and dropped overboard. It was the burial at sea that the old one-eyed sea dog had requested.

His final words could simply have been dismissed as the ravings of a dying man. But sailors are a superstitious lot. Pay's old cabin was allowed to remain vacant for three voyages. But facilities aboard the *Monongahela* were cramped, and the cabin could not be allowed to remain empty forever. A young assistant paymaster joined the ship. He had never known his predecessor, and he adopted a superior air to the warnings and fears of the older sailors. He moved into Cabin No. 2 on the port side.

The *Monongahela* was returning to its home port from South America. For several days the voyage was entirely uneventful. Then one evening in April there was a horrible scream from the vicinity of Cabin No. 2. The men came running. The cabin door was open, and just outside lay the young assistant paymaster. He had apparently been trying to escape from the room when he fainted.

It was several minutes before he regained consciousness. He began muttering, "Wet and horrible. Horrible!"

When he had recovered sufficiently, the young man was asked what had caused him to collapse.

"I was sound asleep in my berth," he said. "I woke up feeling cold and clammy. I felt as if there were something wet right next to me. And there was this awful smell. I lit the lamp, pulled back the covers and found a corpse in my berth with me. It had a red beard, and seemed to be staring at me with one open eye. There was seaweed in its hair and beard. It was horrible, horrible." He began to tremble violently.

Fearfully some of the men entered Cabin No. 2. It was with great relief that they saw the berth was empty. But they were not at all reassured when they found that the blankets were wet and there was seaweed on the mattress.

CHAPTER TWELVE

The Apparition in the Cabin

All too often accounts of ghosts are vague or second-hand or the result of hearsay or tradition rather than firsthand experience. The really good first-person account of a ghost sighting by a credible witness is rare. This is one of the best, a believable eye-witness description of meeting a ghost. The account was given by Harold Owen, an English painter and writer. The ghost in this case was Harold's older brother, Wilfred, whose poems about the First World War were to become very famous. But Wilfred never lived long enough to enjoy his fame. He was killed on November 4, 1918, just one week before the war finally ended.

Wilfred was an officer in the army serving on the

western front. Harold was in the navy. When the war ended, Harold was aboard the light cruiser HMS *Astrea* off the coast of Africa.

Though the ship was in a remote place and information was very slow in reaching it, news of the war's end reached the *Astrea* almost immediately. That set off a great celebration among the officers and men. But somehow the twenty-one-year-old Harold Owen was not able to join in the joyous feelings of the moment. He had been feeling severely depressed for about a week. "I could not enter into any spirit of gaiety. I felt horribly flat, everything else seemed flat."

He was worried about Wilfred and about his younger brother who was also in the army. There had been no bad news, and now that the war was over there was no reason to fear for their safety; yet he did, more acutely than he ever had before. "Something, I knew, was wrong. Monstrous depression clamped hold of me."

It wasn't until a couple of weeks after the end of the war that Harold had what he called "an extraordinary and inexplicable experience." The *Astrea* was anchored off the African coast. It was extremely hot, and Harold was suffering from one of his recurrent bouts of malaria.

"I had gone down to my cabin thinking to write some letters. I drew aside the door curtain and stepped inside and to my amazement saw Wilfred sitting in my chair. I felt shock running through me with appalling force and with it I could feel the blood draining away from my face. I did not rush towards him but walked jerkily into my cabin—all my limbs stiff and slow to respond. I did not sit down but looking at him I spoke quietly:

" 'Wilfred, how did you get here?'

"He did not rise and I saw that he was involuntarily immobile, but his eyes which had never left mine were alive with the familiar look of trying to make me understand. . . . I felt no fear—I had not when I first drew my door curtain and saw him there. . . . All I was conscious of was a sensation of enormous shock and profound astonishment that he should be in my cabin. I spoke again:

" 'Wilfred, how can you be here? It's just not possible. . . .'

"But still he did not speak, but only smiled his most gentle smile. This not speaking did not now as it had done at first seem strange or even unnatural. . . . I loved having him there: I could not, and did not want to try to, understand how he had got there. I was content to accept him; that he was here with me was sufficient. I could not question anything. . . . He was in uniform, and I remember thinking how out of place the khaki looked amongst the cabin furnishings. With this thought I must have turned my eyes away from him; when I looked back my cabin chair was empty. . . .

"I felt the blood run slowly back to my face and looseness into my limbs and with these an overpowering sense of emptiness and absolute loss. . . . I wondered if I had been dreaming, but looking down I saw that I was still standing. Suddenly I felt terribly tired and moving to my bunk I lay down; instantly I went into a deep, oblivious sleep. When I woke up, I knew with absolute certainty that Wilfred was dead. . . .

"The certainty of my conviction of Wilfred's death amounted I realized to absolute knowledge; I could no longer question it. That I had not heard that he had been killed—that weeks had passed since the fighting had stopped—made no difference to me at all; all that could be explained. . . . I accepted his death completely, without hope and without pretense."

Owen's parents were not officially informed of their son's death until the war ended. It was several months before Harold Owen, sitting in his ship off the African coast, received word of Wilfred's death. But by that time it was no surprise; he already knew.

CHAPTER THIRTEEN

A Living "Ghost"

Around the year 1820 Robert Bruce, an experienced seaman, was serving as first mate on a ship that was making a voyage from Liverpool, England, to New Brunswick, Canada. The strange incident occurred after they had been at sea for about six weeks and were somewhere near the Grand Banks of Newfoundland.

One evening, just about sunset, the captain and first mate Bruce were in the captain's cabin. They were making some calculations about the ship's position. For some reason Bruce's calculations weren't working out. He bent over his work and was so absorbed that he didn't notice that the captain had left the cabin and gone up on deck.

When Bruce finally figured out his error, he turned to tell the captain what he had done. But the man hunched over the captain's table made no reply. Bruce got up and began to cross to the captain's table. As he did so, the figure raised its head. It was not the captain at all, but a complete stranger!

The man looked directly at him and held out a small slate, on which something had been written. Bruce was no coward, but this sight suddenly filled him with such apprehension that he did not question the stranger, but rushed up on deck to find the captain.

The captain was on the bridge, and when he saw Bruce approaching he said, "Why, Mr. Bruce, whatever is the matter? You look as if you have seen a ghost."

Hesitantly Bruce told the captain what he had seen. The captain was more than skeptical. "Mr. Bruce, have you taken leave of your senses?"

"No, sir, I assure you there is someone unknown sitting at your desk in the cabin."

The captain replied, quite reasonably, that such a thing was impossible, for they had been at sea for six weeks, and there could not possibly be a stranger aboard. But Bruce was insistent. The captain knew his mate to be a good officer and a man of sound judgment, not given to fancies or practical jokes. So he made the obvious suggestion that they should go down to the cabin and find out if anyone was there.

When they reached the cabin, they found it empty, just as the captain assumed that they would. But Bruce was still insisting that he had seen someone there. Then Bruce noticed something; the slate that the stranger had been holding out was on the captain's table. And there was writing on it. In plain bold letters were the words, "Steer to the nor'west."

The captain's temper was starting to heat up, for he began to suspect that his mate was playing an elaborate but not very funny practical joke on him. Bruce insisted that he was doing nothing of the sort. "On my word, sir. It would not be my idea of a joke either. I have told you the exact truth, sir. I know no more of this writing than you do, sir."

The captain thought for a moment. Then he picked up another slate, handed it to his first mate and said, "Write the words, 'Steer to the nor'west.' "

Bruce did as he was told. The captain then carefully compared the handwriting on the two slates. It was clear to him that they were totally different.

The captain then called for the second mate and ordered him to write the words on the slate. The second mate, who had no idea what was going on and thought that his captain might be losing his mind, obeyed anyway. Once again the two handwritings were completely different.

"Someone must have written these words," said the captain. "And I intend to find out who is trying to make a fool of us. Every man on the ship who can write shall come here and write these words. We will soon find out who is responsible. We'll begin with the steward. Call him up, Mr. Bruce. God help the man who thinks he can play this dangerous kind of joke with me!"

So the steward came and wrote the words. But the handwriting was not his. There were only a few other members of the crew who could write, so it didn't take long for the captain to realize that he was not able to solve the mystery.

Though the captain was quite sure that no one could have stowed away and remained hidden for six weeks, he ordered the ship to be thoroughly searched anyway. The search, of course, turned up nothing.

The captain paced up and down on the deck, while Bruce stood by patiently. Finally the captain turned to his mate and said, "Do you believe in ghosts?"

"Why no, sir," said the mate, "though I have met many who do."

"Nor do I," said the captain. "Yet those words must mean something. Just by way of experiment, what would you say if we did what the message instructed us to do?"

"In your place that is what I would do, sir," Bruce agreed. "At worst we shall only lose a few hours."

So the necessary order was given, and at about 3:00 P.M. the following day the lookout reported an iceberg nearly dead ahead. When the captain and the mate trained their spyglasses on the iceberg, they saw a ship very close to it. As they came nearer, it became clear that the vessel had been frozen into the ice. Soon they were able to make out people waving frantically to them from the deck of the trapped ship.

"Do you imagine, Mr. Bruce, that Providence has sent us this way to assist a ship that has run afoul of an iceberg?" said the captain.

"If that man sitting at your desk was Providence, or sent by Providence," replied the mate, "then I should say yes. We certainly would not have found this ship if we had not obeyed the instructions on the slate."

A boat was sent out to contact the stranded vessel. What had happened was soon known. The trapped ship was from Quebec and bound for Liverpool. She had about fifty passengers on board and had been frozen in the ice for several weeks. The ship itself had nearly been destroyed, and the food was almost gone. Those aboard had practically given up all hope of rescue. Several of the passengers had already died from exposure.

As the survivors were being transferred to the rescue vessel, one of them collapsed from exhaustion as he reached the deck. Bruce rushed forward to support him, but when he got a look at the man, the mate himself nearly fell over. He realized that he was looking into the face of the man who had written "Steer to the nor'-west."

After the survivors had been taken care of, Bruce told the captain about the man. They found him resting below deck.

Somewhat apologetically the captain asked the man if he would participate in a little experiment. "I hope, sir, you will not think that my mate and I are trifling with you if I ask you to write a few words on this slate."

The man was clearly puzzled, but replied, "How can

I refuse to do anything you request, no matter how strange the request may seem at this moment. What shall I write, sir?"

The captain said, "Please write 'Steer to the nor'-west.' "

The man did as asked, and the writing was compared to that on the original slate. They were identical. The captain then explained to the puzzled man what had happened and why he had been asked to write those words on a slate.

After hearing the story, the man described how, at the time Bruce saw the stranger at the captain's table, he had fallen into a deep sleep. Indeed, some of his fellow passengers feared that he had died. But when he awoke a few hours later, he had a firm conviction that they would be rescued the next day. He had dreamed of what the rescue vessel would look like, and it corresponded exactly to the ship that did in fact rescue them.

He had not dreamed of writing a message on the slate, but when he came aboard the vessel everything had seemed strangely familiar to him.

"It is all a puzzle to me," he concluded.

CHAPTER FOURTEEN

The Ghost That Pointed to the Sky

In 1850 Captain Aldridge of the Royal Navy was given command of a vessel called the *Asp*. The ship was an old one and was being refitted as a survey vessel to help map Britain's inland waterways. He commanded the *Asp* for over ten years and kept a careful record of what took place aboard her. He had a hint of what was to come even before he sailed.

When he went to take possession of the *Asp,* the superintendent of the dockyard said to him, "Do you know, sir, your ship is said to be haunted, and I don't know if you will get any of the dockyard men to work on her."

Captain Aldridge smiled and replied, "I don't care for

ghosts, and dare say I shall get her to rights fast enough."

He did get enough workmen to do the repairs, though they all told him the *Asp* was bad luck, and he should give up on it. But in the end the work was done, and one evening Captain Aldridge was sitting in his cabin with another officer when he heard all sorts of strange noises, "such as would be caused by a drunken man or a person staggering about," coming from one of the other cabins. But when the cabin was searched, it was found to be empty.

That was just the first of a long series of noisy disturbances aboard the *Asp*. Wrote Captain Aldridge: "After this evening, the noises became very frequent, varying in kind and degree. Sometimes it was as though the seats and lockers were being banged about, sometimes it sounded as though decanters and tumblers were being clashed together. During these disturbances the vessel was lying more than a mile offshore."

One night he distinctly heard someone run into one of the cabins, and this time he was sure he had trapped the ghost. He had one of his officers guard the cabin door with a sword. "If anyone attempts to escape cut him down. I will stand the consequences," he told the man.

The captain then proceeded to search every inch of the cabin, but could find nothing to account for the noises. "I declare solemnly that never did I feel more certain of anything in my life than that I should find a man there. So there was nothing to be done but to repeat for the hundredth time, 'Well, it is the ghost again!' "

A short time later the sightings began. "One night . . . I was awoke by the quartermaster calling me and begging me to come on deck as the look-out man had rushed to the lower deck saying that a figure of a lady was standing on the paddle box pointing with her finger to Heaven. Feeling angry, I told him to send the look-out man on deck again and keep him there till daybreak, but in attempting to carry my orders into execution the man went into violent convulsions, and the result was I had to go myself upon the deck and remain there till morning."

The apparition appeared frequently after that, and there were voices, too. One day the only man aboard was the steward. He was climbing down the companion ladder when he "was spoken to by an unseen voice. He immediately fell down with fright, and I found his appearance so altered that I really scarcely knew him!"

As the story of the ghost on the *Asp* became generally known, Captain Aldridge had an increasingly difficult time finding and holding a crew. Men would ask to be discharged, "all telling me the same tale, namely that at night they saw the transparent figure of a lady pointing with her finger up to Heaven."

The haunting came to an abrupt and unexpected end in 1857. The ship was in the dock at Pembroke for repairs. All the crew had gone, but a sentry near the ship saw the pointing ghost step from the ship to the shore and walk toward him. The sentry raised his musket and shouted, "Who goes there?" The ghost didn't answer and didn't stop. She walked right through the musket, which the sentry dropped immediately as he ran for safety in the guard house. The ghost was spotted by a second sentry, who fired at it to no effect. The figure then glided past a third sentry, who was standing near the ruins of an old church. The man "watched her, or it, mount the top of a grave in the old churchyard, point with her finger to Heaven, and then stand till she vanished from his sight."

After that the ghost was never seen again aboard the *Asp,* nor were there any more unexplained noises or voices.

Captain Aldridge investigated the background of his ship and reported: "Some years previously to my having her the *Asp* had been engaged as a mail boat. After one of her trips, the passengers having all disembarked, the stewardess on going into the ladies' cabin found a beautiful girl with her throat cut lying in one of the sleeping berths quite dead! How she came by her death no one could tell and, though, of course, strict investigations were commenced neither who she was nor where she came from or anything about her was ever discovered."

There was a great deal of talk, and the vessel was taken out of service for some years, then it was refitted and turned over to Captain Aldridge in the hope that its reputation would be forgotten.

At the end of his careful account, the captain concludes: "Here ends my tale, which I have given in all truth. Much as I know one gets laughed at for believing in ghost stories you are welcome to make what use you please with this true account of the apparition on board the *Asp*."

CHAPTER FIFTEEN

Phantom Ships

Of all the ghostly legends of the sea the most famous by far is that of the *Flying Dutchman*. The story has been told and retold in many different forms for many years. Details sometime vary, but basically the story is this:

While sailing around the Cape of Good Hope, the southern tip of Africa, a ship encounters a terrible storm. The crew begs the captain to put them into a safe harbor. Not only does the captain refuse, he laughs at their fears and tells them that he is afraid of nothing on earth or in heaven.

The storm grows worse, and a glowing form appears on the deck. The crew is terrified, but as usual the captain shows neither fear nor respect. He says to the form, "Who wants a peaceful passage? I don't; I'm asking nothing from you. Clear out unless you want your brains blown out."

The captain then draws his pistol and fires at the form, but the pistol explodes in his hand. Then the form pronounces a curse on the captain. He is doomed to sail forever without rest. "And since it is your delight to torment sailors you shall torment them, for you shall be the evil spirit of the sea. Your ship shall bring misfortune to all who sight it."

Traditionally the captain has been called Cornelius Vanderdecken, a Dutch sailor who was supposed to have lived in the sixteenth century. There is, however, no record of a Captain Vanderdecken. The legend may have started with a somewhat later Dutch sea captain named Bernard Fokke. Fokke was a daring and skilled mariner. Some of the voyages he made were so remarkable that it was rumored he had supernatural aid. Fokke's ship was lost at sea. Those are just the sort of circumstances that can give rise to a legend.

There have been many reported sightings of the *Flying Dutchman* over the centuries. The best known was penned by a blunt, no-nonsense man who wrote in the log of the English ship *Baccante* in July 1881:

"The *Flying Dutchman* crossed our bows. A strange red light, as of a phantom ship all aglow, in the midst of which light the masts, spars and sails of a brig two hundred yards distant stood up in strong relief. . . . On arriving there, no vestige nor any sign whatever of any material ship was to be seen either near or right away to the horizon, the night being clear and the sea calm. Thirteen persons altogether saw her."

The man who wrote those words was Prince George of England. He was later to become King George V. As prince and king, George was never known to be a fanciful or imaginative man. If the phantom ship was an illusion, it must have been a very convincing one.

The prince himself did not suffer any bad luck as the result of the encounter, but the first of the men to have sighted the ship fell to his death from the mast. The admiral aboard the *Baccante* became ill and died shortly after the voyage ended.

While the *Flying Dutchman* is the most famous of the phantom ships, it is by no means the only one. According to some legends Captain Vanderdecken's *Flying Dutchman* is one phantom and Captain Fokke's ship is another.

The three-masted schooner *Lady Lovibond* went down in a storm with all hands aboard off the coast of England in 1748. But the vessel has been seen at fifty-year intervals ever since. Her next scheduled appearance is 1998.

Captain Kidd's ship is said to still sail around the New England coast, with the old pirate in an eternal search for the treasure that he buried somewhere, but that no one can seem to locate. Another pirate ship, that of Jean Laffite, has been reported in the Gulf of Mexico off Galveston, Texas. That is where Laffite's ship is believed to have sunk in the 1820s. In the nineteenth century an American ship named *Dash* vanished at sea. The ghost of that ship is supposed to return to port every so often to pick up the souls of crew members' families after they have died.

Ghost ships are not limited to the sea either. The Great Lakes, which are notoriously stormy and treacherous, have more than their share of vanished ships—and attendant ghost tales. The best known of the Great Lakes phantoms is the *Griffin,* property of the great French explorer Robert Cavelier La Salle. She was built at Niagara, five miles above the falls, and first set sail on August 7, 1679. The *Griffin* was the largest ship to sail the Great Lakes up to that time and according to legend, the Indians had placed a curse upon it.

La Salle left the *Griffin* at Green Bay, Wisconsin, at the end of the first leg of her journey. He set out by canoe down the St. Joseph River, searching for a river route to the Mississippi. The *Griffin* sailed from Green Bay on September 18, 1679, bound back for Niagara. She never made it. She simply "sailed through a crack in the ice"—or so the legend goes. But on some nights lake men have reported seeing the ghostly form of the *Griffin* looming out of the fog.

The most celebrated of all phantom ships in the United States is the *Palatine.* She left Holland in 1752 packed with immigrants bound for Philadelphia. But a storm blew her off course, and her crew mutinied. The terrified passengers were totally helpless for days.

Two days after Christmas the ship ran aground on the rocks near Block Island, off the coast of Rhode Island. When the storm abated, local fishermen removed the surviving passengers, but then attacked and looted the wreck.

After they had stripped everything of value from the ship, they set her afire and watched her drift out into the open sea. It was only then that they realized that not everyone had been taken off the ship. A woman driven half mad by the hardships had hidden somewhere and now appeared from her hiding place. The fishermen watched in horror as she stood screaming on the deck until the flames consumed her.

Ever since then visitors to Block Island have reported the sight of a burning ship. Locally it is known as the *Palatine* light.

One final phantom is not a ship, but a voice. Since 1875 people along the Mississippi River near Vicksburg, Mississippi, have from time to time reported that they heard a woman screaming for help somewhere on the river. In most cases the screams are followed by words in French: "Aidez-moi au nom de Dieu, les hommes me blessent!" ("Help me in the name of God, the men are hurting me!")

Those along the river have linked the voice to something that occurred in June 1874. The riverboat *Iron Mountain* set out from Vicksburg for New Orleans carrying fifty-seven passengers and towing a string of barges. Somewhere on the voyage the big paddle-wheel steamer simply vanished. The barges were later found bobbing in the water. The towropes had been slashed in two. Hundreds of miles of riverbottom were dragged, but no trace of the ship was ever found.

One of the most plausible explanations offered for the disappearance was that the ship was attacked by river pirates, who still operated quite freely for years after the Civil War. The *Iron Mountain* would certainly have offered a tempting target.

On the passenger list were several Creole women who spoke French. Could the ghostly voice be that of one of the pirates' victims?

CHAPTER SIXTEEN

Haunted Ships You Can Visit

There is no guarantee that if you take an ocean voyage around the Cape of Good Hope, you will see the *Flying Dutchman*. Nor can you be sure if you spend the summer on Block Island, you will spot the *Palatine* light. But there are a couple of haunted ships that you can visit with relative ease. You may not actually see any ghosts during your visit. Probably you won't. But you will be able to see a place where ghostly events are supposed to have taken place regularly.

The *Constellation,* once flagship of the U.S. Navy, is on display at a pier in Baltimore Harbor. It is open to the public and can be visited by anyone for a small fee. The ship has a long and distinguished history. It was built in

1797 as the first man-of-war in the U.S. fleet. Time and changes in naval warfare finally caught up with the *Constellation,* and several attempts were made to decommission her and pass the proud old name on to a new ship. But something always happened. Finally she wound up forgotten and rotting in the harbor at Newport, Rhode Island. President Franklin D. Roosevelt made an attempt to have her restored in 1940, but before the project got started the United States was deep into World War II. It wasn't until the 1950s that the private citizens in Baltimore raised the funds to have the ship taken to the harbor there and restored as a tourist attraction. It remains one of the chief attractions of Baltimore's rebuilt harbor area today.

Now for the ghosts. The one reported most frequently is an old sailor identified as Neil Harvey. He has appeared to visitors to the *Constellation* wearing the uniform of his day and is sometimes mistaken as a costumed attendant. Harvey was a gunner who had fallen asleep while on duty and was then strapped to the barrel of his gun and blown to bits as punishment for the offense. A second ghost is that of Thomas Truxtun, the captain who ordered that harsh punishment. There is some speculation that Captain Truxtun's spirit cannot rest because he feels guilty about what he had done. The execution of Harvey took place sometime between 1795 and 1802. Another ghost reported on this historic ship is that of a cabin boy who died aboard in 1822.

A more contemporary set of ghosts has been associated with the ocean liner the *Queen Mary*. This great ship made its maiden voyage from Southampton, England, to New York in 1936. During World War II she served honorably and effectively as a troop carrier. After the war she went back to the business of ferrying passengers across the Atlantic in high style and luxury. But in the end the great ocean liners could not compete with aircraft, so in 1967, after 1,001 crossings of the Atlantic, she was retired. There was, however, so much history and romance attached to the great ship that she wasn't simply junked. She was moved to the port of Long Beach in California, where she is permanently berthed and serves as a tourist attraction and a hotel with 390 staterooms and four restaurants. In the early 1990s considerable deterioration had been detected in the ship's structure, so before you visit you better check to see if she is open or closed for repairs.

With a ship that has carried such a large range of passengers over so long a period of time, it is not surprising that a great variety of ghostly events have been recorded.

The most persistent reports go back to the great liner's days as a troop carrier. In October 1942 the ocean liner was zigzagging to confuse German submarines when she slammed into an escorting cruiser, HMS *Curaco*. Some 300 sailors died as a result of the accident. After the ship was retired and while it was being prepared as a tourist attraction, workmen reported hearing voices and sounds of rushing water in the part of the ship that had been affected by the accident. The workmen had known nothing about the accident, for it had largely been kept from the public by wartime censorship. Using a tape recorder, investigators managed to catch what sounds like water in that area.

People who work on the ship report that stateroom doors open and close mysteriously and that the sound of the engine can be heard, though the ship no longer has a working engine. Visitors say they have heard the sounds of keys rattling, chains dragging and the happier noises of a party and shouts and splashing in the pool area.

One security sergeant reported an unusual experience:

"I was standing alone on the stairs to the swimming pool when out of the side of my eye I saw a woman in her forties or fifties wearing a striped, old-fashioned-style bathing suit. She was poised as if about to dive into the pool, which was empty. When I turned full face to stop her, she was gone." Others have reported seeing a similar figure. A woman once did drown in the ship's pool.

This same security officer also said, "I was going up the second escalator when suddenly I felt I was being stared at. There was a man on the step behind me. He had black hair and a black beard and was wearing dark blue coveralls. I stepped aside to let him pass and he was gone."

Another frequently reported apparition is "The

Woman in White," an evening-gowned figure who drapes herself over the piano in the ship's salon.

Those who work in the restaurants on the berthed *Queen Mary* have noted that utensils and food disappear at an alarming rate. In the kitchen dishes are moved around, and lights go on and off mysteriously. Those who know the history of the ship suspect that all of these occurrences may be traced back to something that happened while the luxury liner was on wartime duty. Back then a chief cook aboard the ship was so bad at his job that the sailors aboard threatened a mutiny unless he was replaced. The situation was so serious that the captain actually had to call for help from another ship. In the meantime someone had taken the cook and thrown him into the oven. The unfortunate man died as a result of his burns.